Margaret, Pirate Queen

Written by Marsha S. Tennant
with Dub Sutton
Illustrated by Amy Chapman

ISBN 978-1-936352-39-5
1-936352-39-7

Published by Mirror Publishing
Milwaukee, WI 53214

Printed in the USA.

This book is dedicated to my daughter, Alice, who brought
Margaret and Maverick
into my life (Marsha Tennant, 2010)
And
To Stormy, the best dog and companion I ever had.
(Dub Sutton, 2010)
And
To the students in Karen Campbell's third grade class at
North Myrtle Beach Elementary, South Carolina (2007-08)
who taught us the magic of pirate doggie dialogue and
the courage to bring the story to life
Marsha, Dub and Amy (2010)

The porch was Margaret's favorite place to take an afternoon nap and dream her pirate adventures on the Coastal Carolina waters. She opened her eyes and the little backyard pond became the lagoon where The Howling Queen, her schooner, began to appear out of the mist.

Margaret stepped off the porch and greeted her crew. Margaret wanted to be like Anne Bonny, the famous female pirate. Both were known for their BLING and taking booty from their enemies.

Margaret swaggered up the gangplank of The Howling Queen, barking orders. "Look lively, you sea dogs. Prepare to set sail! We will do battle before the sun sets! Yum...shrimp for supper tonight!"

Her first mate, Mad Maverick, towered above the crew. He had to wear an eye patch over one very ugly eye. He drooled when he was excited which made him look like his name. He stood beside her watching the crew prepare to launch.

He had his hand on the cutlass he carried in his belt. Mad Maverick loved a good fight. "Hoist the colors, ready for battle, mates," he bellowed.

A ship, The Bulldog Bandit, lay on the horizon.

Margaret heard there was a bounty of shrimp to be taken. Churchill was the captain and had a skeleton crew. The battle would be easy for The Howling Queen.

Margaret lifted her nose, getting a whiff of shrimp and gunpowder. "Ahhhwhooowwww...Victory will be mine today!"

The frightened crew of The Bulldog Bandit recognized the howl. Margaret, Mad Maverick, and her crew boarded the enemy ship. Churchill and his motley crew fought bravely but were no match for the skill of The Howling Queen. Swords clashed and the enemy crew was quickly defeated.

With streams of drool pouring from his chin, Mad Maverick jumped on the main cannon of The Bulldog Bandit and screamed out in rage, "Surrender or die. The choice is yours!"

He waved his cutlass! There would be no challenge to his demands. He ordered the captured crew to load The Howling Queen with the bounty of shrimp.

Under the Pirate's Code, the captured crew had the choice of joining up with the victor or be exiled to an island. Some of the crew joined up with The Howling Queen. Churchill and a few of his loyal mates chose nearby Skull Island. Margaret was fearless, but not heartless, so she honored the code.

The Howling Queen sailed all night under a full Carolina moon. The reward for the crew was a supper of succulent shrimp. They all laughed and shared stories of the day's battle. By daylight they would arrive at the Charleston Market ready to sell their bounty.

The next morning while the crew was unloading The Howling Queen, Margaret put on her finest BLING and called for Mad Maverick to join her on her trip to the market. She and Mad Maverick strolled down the gangplank. They were surprised to see former mates hanging around the dock.

"Ahoy, Pirate Queen, good to see you again," Calico Kody yelled. He had a reputation for cheating and stealing.

Phoebe screamed in excitement, "Let me go with you, Pirate Queen. I want to be a sea dog, too."

Mad Maverick began to drool again. He smelled trouble with these scallywags hanging around. "Jack and Tanner, what are you doing in Charleston? I thought you both were on The Flying Mackerel."

"Got kicked off. It was that or walk the plank," Jack mumbled.

Tanner hung his head in shame and spoke in a low voice, "Shouldn't have listened to Jack."

"They stole shrimp from the captain, Crazy Quint," Millie barked. She was laughing at the thought of those two being caught.

"Hummmmm....knew there was a reason you didn't trust them, Pirate Queen," Mad Maverick whispered as he wiped the drool from his chin.

"Glad they aren't on The Howling Queen anymore. I never liked any of them. Bet we will see them again - always do."

Margaret did some shopping at the famous Charleston Market. She was always looking for new BLING to add to her image. Mad Maverick bought supplies and food to ready the crew for sailing on the morning tide.

The Howling Queen set sail the next morning with a strong tailwind pushing them out into inlet waters. Margaret swaggered up on deck and addressed her crew. "Sea dogs, we will strike Dolphin Island next. There are rumors of many treasures on sloops and schooners. We can attack at night, under the cover of darkness."

The crew nodded their heads in agreement. Mad Maverick thought it was a grand idea. He knew they had a score to settle with pirate ships around Dolphin Island. Some of the pirates had betrayed the Pirate Queen and her crew in the past.

"We have waited to get even and now we will," he drooled in excitement.

"Patience, Mad Maverick. We will get our revenge," Margaret said in a determined voice.

"I am glad you are our captain," Mad Maverick said in admiration.

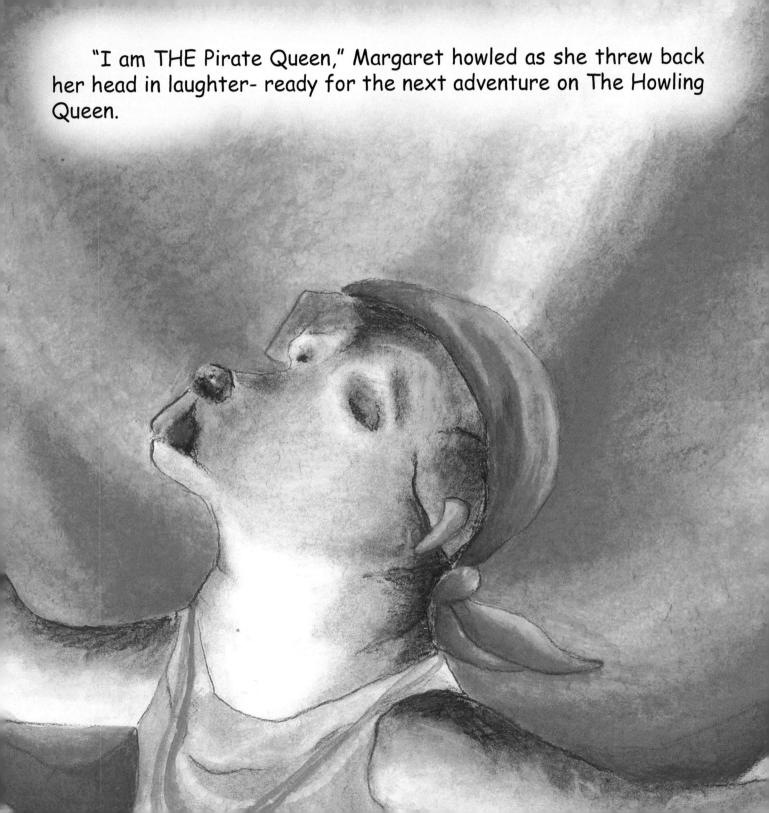

"I am THE Pirate Queen," Margaret howled as she threw back her head in laughter- ready for the next adventure on The Howling Queen.

The End

CPSIA information can be obtained
at www.ICGtesting.com
Printed in the USA
BVHW090720280619
552186BV00001B/1/P